ADVENTURES IN COLONIAL AMERICA

ADVENTURES IN COLONIAL AMERICA

JOURNEY TO MONTICELLO

Traveling in Colonial Times

by James E. Knight

Illustrated by George Guzzi

Troll Associates

Library of Congress Cataloging in Publication Data

Knight, James E.
    Journey to Monticello.

    Summary: Follows a young man as he uses
different modes of transportation to make the long
difficult trip from Massachusetts to Virginia in
the spring of 1775.
    1. United States—Description and travel—To
1783—Juvenile literature. [1. United States—
Description and travel—To 1783. 2. Transportation
—History] I. Guzzi, George, ill. II. Title.
E163.K64   917.3 '042   81-23156
ISBN 0-89375-736-5   AACR2
ISBN 0-89375-737-3 (pbk.)

10   9   8   7   6   5   4   3   2   1

ADVENTURES IN COLONIAL AMERICA

JOURNEY TO MONTICELLO

Traveling in Colonial Times

Troll Associates

It began one rainy April evening in 1775. Young Amos Trumbull was at his home in Braintree, Massachusetts. He had opened a law practice in the city not long before.

Amos heard a loud knock at the door. He was surprised to find John Hancock standing there. Amos knew Mr. Hancock slightly. In fact, he had carried messages for him from time to time.

John Hancock

John Hancock warmed himself before the fire. Then he said, "I will come right to the point, Amos. I need a messenger, and you have proven yourself trustworthy. A packet of important papers must leave for Virginia tonight. The man that usually does this work is ill. Will you take these papers for me, and for our country as well?"

With barely a pause, Amos said that he would.

"Good!" said John Hancock. "I will give you money, of course, for the journey. How you go is your own choice. These papers must be in Mr. Jefferson's hands before he leaves for Philadelphia."

Amos Trumbull could hardly believe it. He was to deliver the papers to Thomas Jefferson at Monticello in Virginia. Jefferson would need time to study them before leaving for the Continental Congress, which was to be held in Philadelphia in May. There would be British patrols along the route to Virginia. The mission, Hancock warned him, must be kept secret.

Amos packed a small valise and dressed warmly.
Ahead of him was a long, hard journey through many
colonies.

He set out on foot for Dedham, a town about fifteen
miles away. He walked briskly through the melting spring
snow. "I must reach Dedham by four o'clock in the
morning," he thought, "or I shall miss the Boston stagecoach." If Amos missed the Boston stage, he knew he
would have to wait for two days. There were only three
stagecoaches each week.

Shortly after midnight, he reached the Neponset River. The small log bridge had been washed out. Amos was forced to wade across, and he continued his journey in wet shoes.

Tired and cold, he reached Dedham just in time to see the stage wagon clatter toward him. It was little more than a box on springs. The stage could hold eleven passengers and a driver. There were four benches inside, but the first three had no backs. So everyone wanted the rear bench, where they could lean against the back of the wagon. Amos sat down on the third bench. The rear bench was already filled. "I'm lucky to get a seat at all, I suppose," he thought. The driver cracked his whip at the four horses, and the journey began.

The wagon rumbled down Boston Post Road, the only major route between Boston and New York City. From time to time, Amos patted the papers in his greatcoat pocket. He had taken the time to sew the pocket shut. He was determined not to lose so important a package.

"Uncomfortable, uncomfortable," muttered the stout man sitting next to Amos. Amos had to agree. He began to regret not taking his own horse. But his horse would have tired, and he would have had to get another. No, the stage wagon was the right choice. At least for now.

By afternoon, Amos felt as if every bone in his body had been broken. The wagon seemed to hit each stone in the rough road. Bags and parcels cramped the passengers' legs. Everyone shivered as the cold spring air blew through the leather curtains on three sides of the wagon. "At least it's not snowing," thought Amos.

But when they reached Attleboro, it began to rain. The raindrops blew into the cramped wagon, and soon everyone was soaked. Everyone was hungry by this time, too. But the driver would not stop for lunch. Wagon drivers, in those days, often ran their wagons as a captain runs a ship. In fact, the passengers called the driver "captain."

By dusk, they were a few miles out of Pawtucket. Amos was looking forward to spending the night there. But, suddenly, the wagon came to a dead stop. All the passengers were thrown off their benches.

The driver jumped out and began yelling. "Let's go, gentlemen! We've hit a muddy rut. The whole wagon is tipping. All lean to the right, or we shall overturn. Lean! Lean!" Everyone leaned far to the right. The wagon righted itself.

The weary group reached Pawtucket about ten o'clock that evening. Amos could scarcely stand up as he stepped from the wagon. They had been on the road for nearly twenty hours!

The owner of the wayside inn was a large, friendly man. He offered them a poor supper of salt pork and cornbread. To Amos, it tasted marvelous.

That night Amos slept in a tiny area with no window, no door, and no fireplace. But he was too tired to care. He crawled into the four-poster bed without undressing.

Moments later—or so it seemed—Amos was awakened. A lantern was shining in his face, and a voice said, "Wake up, sir! Your stage leaves in twenty minutes." It was three o'clock in the morning.

By candlelight, Amos splashed water on his face from a washbasin. He checked to make sure the papers were safe, and put on his greatcoat. Soon the stagecoach was bumping south again in the dark.

Sometime later the driver pulled up at a small inn. "Breakfast!" he yelled. Amos and the others ate as much as they could. They knew they would not eat again that day until after dark.

On the road once more, Amos could glimpse the Narragansett Bay on his right. A brisk wind was churning the water into whitecaps.

Another miserable day of travel passed. The wagon reached Newport about nine o'clock that evening. Amos was tired, cold, and hungry. He was also dirty. Outside of Bristol, the wagon had become stuck in the mud again. This time everyone had to get out and help the driver lift the wagon back on the road. Then they had to free the horses from the mud.

That night Amos slept at the Cross Keys Inn. It was somewhat better lodgings than the night before. But Amos slept uneasily. He truly dreaded the next day. He had to take two ferries across Narragansett Bay to the mainland. Amos was afraid of water, for he could not swim a stroke!

When he saw the ferryboat, Amos was more uneasy than ever. It was just large enough to carry the stage

wagon, the horses, and the passengers. It was attached by pulleys to a rope stretched across the water. The rope kept the wagon from being swept out to sea.

A northwest wind blew hard across the bay, as the ferry moved slowly over the choppy water. Waves sprayed the boat and drenched everyone. After what seemed a very long time, the ferry reached shore. Even the bumpy stage wagon seemed a relief to Amos when they were on the road once more.

"We'll reach Stonington in Connecticut by nightfall," the driver said.

"How far is that?" Amos asked.

"Some twenty miles," said the driver.

As they bumped along the Post Road, it began to rain hard. By four o'clock that afternoon, the road was a mass of slippery mud. Once more the stage lurched off the road and stopped.

Everyone hopped out again and began to push and pull and tug. But it was no use. They could not budge the wagon.

"Help will be here tomorrow," said the driver. "We'll just have to wait."

"How far is it to Stonington?" Amos asked. He knew he could not wait until tomorrow.

"A good eight-mile walk," said the driver.

Tired, wet, and dirty, Amos set out alone on the Post Road. He bundled his greatcoat about him and patted the papers in his pocket. With his valise in his hand, he turned and waved to the stage wagon. "Good luck," he called.

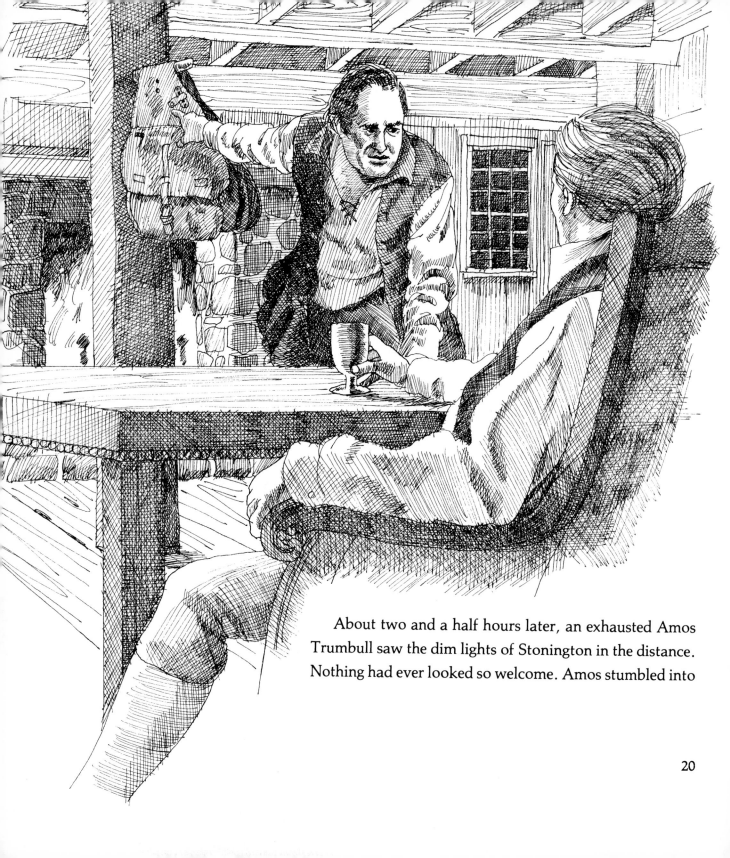

About two and a half hours later, an exhausted Amos Trumbull saw the dim lights of Stonington in the distance. Nothing had ever looked so welcome. Amos stumbled into an inn, which also served as the post office. After he changed his wet clothes, he ate a huge supper. Later, he sat before the fire and talked to the innkeeper.

"I must reach New York as soon as possible," Amos told him. "What do you suggest I do?"

"We may be able to help each other," said the innkeeper. "See that?" He pointed to two saddlebags of mail and some stacks of letters. Each letter was folded twice and sealed with a bit of wax. "I'll solve your problem if you'll solve mine," he continued. "The regular postrider is sick. But his horse is fresh. If you'll deliver these letters to the inns and stores along the way, you can ride as far as New Haven. You'll have to change horses at Saybrook. What do you say?"

"I say yes, indeed. Thank you, sir," said Amos.

Early the next morning, Amos threw the saddlebags on the horse and was off again on the Post Road. By mid-afternoon he had reached the ferry at the Thames River in New London. Forty minutes later, he was on the opposite shore, riding hard for Saybrook.

21

At dawn the next day, Amos received a fresh horse and was on his way again. Another ferry—and he crossed the wide Connecticut River. Hours of hard riding lay ahead. But by dusk he could see the lights of New Haven. He delivered the rest of his letters to the post office, and took a room at the inn.

In the early morning, he boarded a stage wagon. He was traveling once again on the Boston Post Road. The weather was dry, and the stage made good time. After they crossed the Quinnipiac River, they stopped at Stratford. Then they had to cross the Housatonic. "I hope this is the last river," Amos thought to himself. But it was not. After they passed through Fairfield, they continued to Norwalk where they had to ferry across the Norwalk River. By that night they had reached Stamford on the Long Island Sound.

Amos awoke the next morning eager to reach New York. The stage passed through the villages of Rye, New Rochelle, and Mount Vernon. At last, they traveled down

a long slope and were in sight of Manhattan Island. They clattered across King's Bridge and on through the countryside of Manhattan, with its taverns and large estates.

"New York at last," said Amos as they rolled down the main thoroughfare known as Broadway. That night was spent in lodgings at the tip of the island, near the unfinished fort called the Battery.

"How might I cross the North, or Hudson, river to the Jerseys, sir?" Amos asked the innkeeper early the next morning.

"A westward walk to the ferry docks should do it," the man replied. "Two ferries a day leave for Paulus Hook, or Jersey City, as some say. But I must warn you, sir. The crossing is made in an open boat. It is very dangerous when the water is rough."

Amos felt his stomach grow queasy. But what choice did he have?

Valise in hand and wearing his greatcoat, Amos headed for the docks. On the way he passed a small group of British soldiers marching south to the fort. He felt for the packet of papers sewed into his pocket. They were safe.

When Amos reached the Hudson River, he could see a good north wind whipping the water into choppy waves.

One of the ferryboats had just arrived from Paulus Hook, and the passengers were soaked to the skin. They all looked miserable and not a little frightened.

"This is not for me," thought Amos. He set out to find another way to cross. He met an old Dutch fisherman farther up the waterfront. For three shillings, the fisherman agreed to take Amos across the Hudson in his wide-beamed sloop. The trip took two hours. Amos was soaked to the skin by the spray. But he decided it was still better than the ferryboat.

"Can you tell me the way to Philadelphia?" Amos asked the fisherman.

"It's a two-mile walk to the ferry," said the fisherman.

"Another ferry," Amos thought.

"A scow will take you across the Hackensack River," continued the fisherman. "From there you go to Newark, where you had best spend the night."

Amos did as the fisherman instructed. He arrived in Newark on foot that evening. After he had found lodgings, he made a decision. It was now well into April— eight weary days had passed since he had started. He must make better time in order to reach Monticello before Mr. Jefferson left for Philadelphia.

So the next morning, Amos bought a fine, strong horse and set off across Jersey. It was a hard ride, and Amos was exhausted when he arrived in the little college town of Princeton.

From Princeton, Amos galloped the few miles to Trenton, by the Delaware River. He boarded a large flatboat loaded with flour for Philadelphia. The captain of the flatboat was about eighteen years old and very inexperienced. He ran into about half a dozen smaller vessels before they reached the other side.

Amos spent very little time in the city of Philadelphia. But he could not help but notice the bustling activity of the town. Everyone was getting ready for the Continental Congress. And that reminded Amos of his need to hurry.

Amos was startled to hear some gentlemen on a street corner talking of independence from Great Britain. Amos was not a Tory. He was not sympathetic to British rule. But talk of this kind sounded like treason!

That same day, Amos headed down Baltimore Road. He did not know it, but it would be the last good road he would see for the rest of his journey. He passed through Wilmington, and by nightfall had reached the head of Chesapeake Bay.

The next morning brought him to still another ferry. This time he crossed the Susquehanna River to a place called Havre de Grace. By exchanging his horse for a fresh one, he was able to reach Baltimore by dusk.

Now Amos headed for the Potomac River. The trip was miserable, winding endlessly through thick forests. But he finally reached the Potomac. Years later, this spot would become the capital of the United States—Washington, District of Columbia. But when Amos saw it, it was only a swamp on a river called Anacostia. It was practically empty except for a few poor shacks along the water.

If Amos thought his journey was difficult up to now, it was nothing compared to what lay ahead. He had to ride through one hundred miles of stark wilderness. The journey took him three days and two nights—all in pouring rain. The roads were little more than horse paths. In the rain, they turned into rivers of mud. Every few miles, he was stopped by streams or small rivers. He had to lead his horse through the water.

It was now late afternoon of the third day since he had entered this wilderness. Amos had seen no one since his last ferry ride. He was cold and hungry and tired and miserable. He was also lost.

Too tired to go on, even if he knew which direction, Amos dismounted and sat down beneath a tree to rest. At least the rain had stopped. Soon his head began to nod.

Suddenly, someone was shaking his shoulder. "Are you hurt, sir?" the stranger asked.

"No, no," Amos stammered, feeling quickly for the papers in his pocket. "But I am lost. Can you direct me to Mr. Jefferson's house at a place called Monticello?"

"You are indeed in luck, sir," said the man. "I work for Mr. Jefferson. Come, Monticello is but half a mile away."

When they reached Monticello, Amos was more tired and hungry than he had ever been. But even so, he was impressed with the beauty of the grounds. And he marveled at the white columns and dome of the handsome manor house. To think it had been designed and built by Thomas Jefferson himself!

Inside the great house, Amos followed the man through the main entrance hall. Smaller hallways branched off to many rooms. He could see that some parts of the interior were not yet finished.

At last they reached a paneled oak door. The man knocked on it.

"Come in," said a voice.

Amos and the man entered. Inside, a man in his shirt-sleeves sat at a large desk, writing. He ran his big hand through his sandy hair and looked up.

"Your pardon, sir," said Amos's guide. "This gentleman has come all the way from Boston to see you."

"From Boston you say?"

"Just about, Mr. Jefferson," Amos replied. Then he explained his mission and handed over the papers he had brought from John Hancock.

"Thank you," said Thomas Jefferson. "Will you pardon me a moment?" Then he opened the packet and glanced through the papers. He smiled and began to nod as he read.

31

Presently he looked up and said, "I forget my manners, sir. You have traveled a long, hard way. Surely you are weary and are in need of rest and food and dry clothing. You will, of course, dine tonight with my wife and me. And I insist that you stay and rest with us for a few days. I offer you the very best of Monticello. Truly, sir, I appreciate what you have done."

Amos Trumbull never forgot those three days at Monticello. Thomas and Martha Jefferson could not have been more kind or generous.

At dinner one evening, Mr. Jefferson said to him, "Amos, my friend, tell me what you think of as the worst part of your journey."

"Frankly, sir," said Amos, "it is the thought that I must travel all the way back!"